TO READERS AND
FUTURE READERS EVERYWHERE

www.mascotbooks.com

YOJO Presents: Choose to Read

For more information, please contact:
Mascot Books
560 Herndon Parkway #120
Herndon, VA 20170
info@mascotbooks.com

Library of Congress Control Number: 2015937489

CPSIA Code: PRT0515A
ISBN-13: 978-1-63177-164-4

Printed in the United States

He's a big, blue, fuzzy guy who loves to put on hilarious shows for kids. YoJo and his friends have performed *thousands and thousands* of comedy shows. But YoJo's favorite place to perform is elementary schools!

YoJo loves to play and have fun, but he does have some weird habits. For breakfast every day, he eats two buckets of deep-fried clams and chicken feet.

When he takes a bath, he washes in a tub full of
root beer and pickle juice!

But the weirdest thing about YoJo is that he says he doesn't like to read. Isn't that crazy!? Many have tried to talk him into opening up and enjoying a good book, but YoJo will have none of it. He would just rather watch TV and play video games.

One day, YoJo and his friend, Philip, were doing a school science experiment. Philip said, "YoJo, you need to read these instructions before we start mixing chemicals. It's very important that we follow them carefully."

But did YoJo listen to Philip? Of course not! He started mixing all sorts of chemicals just because they made pretty colors.

Philip yelled, "No wait, YoJo! Don't mix the red and the white chemicals! The instructions say not to do that..."

All of a sudden...*WHOOSH!* The red and white chemicals had a bad reaction and YoJo made a huge mess.

"Thanks, YoJo," said Philip after their teacher made them stay after school and clean up.

When YoJo was on the football team, his coach told him, "Okay, YoJo. You're playing quarterback tomorrow for the big game. You've got the talent, but you have to read the playbook. We're trying some new plays, and you have to read up on them."

Yeah, yeah, yeah, thought YoJo. Why bother reading? I'll just throw it when I see somebody open.

The next day, the game was tied 14-14. YoJo's teammate, Lee, came from the bench to talk to YoJo. "Coach says to use the new secret play from the playbook. I'll be your receiver. You know where to throw it!"

"Uhhhh...I guess," said YoJo. But he really had no clue. With three seconds left in the game, YoJo tried to pass it to Lee but couldn't find him. YoJo panicked and threw the ball to someone who wasn't expecting it. The football bounced off their helmet right into the hands of the other team. Interception and touchdown!

YoJo's team ended up losing the big game.

A few days later, YoJo was invited to Cameron's birthday party. Cameron gave YoJo directions to her house. But did YoJo read them? No way! He just drove and drove around. Instead of arriving at Cameron's house, YoJo ended up at the city dump!

No birthday cake for YoJo. No birthday present for Cameron. Cameron was in tears, and all of Cameron's friends at the party were very sad.

The next day at school, Cameron asked YoJo what happened.

YoJo was very embarrassed. "I feel horrible. I got lost. I just didn't want to read your directions and didn't make it. I'm so sorry."

Cameron sighed. "Oh, YoJo. When will you ever learn...
THE MORE YOU READ - THE SMARTER YOU GET?"

And then finally - YoJo had his eureka moment! He thought to himself, *You know, she's right! Why in the world would I choose not to read?! My grades would be better and I could learn about so many things!*

"And you know what, YoJo?" asked Cameron. "Reading is not only very important, but it can be a lot of fun!"

YoJo was stunned. "Reading can be FUN?!?"

"Totally fun! It's not just about homework or instructions. You can read up on...well, on just about anything."

YoJo started thinking again.

...I could read books about pirates and adventures out at sea!

...I could even read cookbooks and learn how to make great food!

...I could read about places around the world and see what life is like in other countries.

...I could read about how rockets travel into space to go to the moon and beyond!

...I could read about anything!

"Where else? Off to the library! I'm going to check out and enjoy some great books!"

This CHOOSE TO READ story is loosely based upon YoJo's award-winning educational comedy show with the same name. The character of YoJo debuted on March 2, 2000 (Read Across America Day) and performs hundreds of "hilariously educational" kids comedy shows every year on many different topics. If you are interested in having YoJo perform an A+ assembly program at your elementary school, please visit his website at www.YoJo.com.

ABOUT THE AUTHOR

Bromley Lowe is the creator and producer of The YoJo Show.
He was a professional mascot with the Baltimore Orioles,
Baltimore Ravens, World Cup Soccer, and a college mascot at
American University in Washington, DC.